Little monsters, and BIG monsters, this is for you!

Thank you so much for showing yourselves to me.—L. B.

For Critters, Whatsits, and Metal Pigs!—B. C.

SIMON & SCHUSTER BOOKS FOR YOUNG READERS
An imprint of Simon & Schuster Children's Publishing Division
1230 Avenue of the Americas, New York, New York 10020
Text copyright © 1998 by Laurie Berkner
Illustrations copyright © 2018 by Ben Clanton
SIMON & SCHUSTER BOOKS FOR YOUNG READERS is a trademark of Simon & Schuster, Inc.
For information about special discounts for bulk purchases, please contact Simon & Schuster Special
Sales at 1-866-506-1949 or business@simonandschuster.com.
The Simon & Schuster Speakers Bureau can bring authors to your live event. For more information
or to book an event, contact the Simon & Schuster Speakers Bureau at 1-866-248-3049 or visit our
website at www.simonspeakers.com.
Book design by Lucy Ruth Cummins
The text for this book was set in VF Sans.
The illustrations for this book were rendered in colored pencil and
watercolor, and assembled and colored digitally.
Manufactured in China
0518 SCP
First Edition
2 4 6 8 10 9 7 5 3 1
Library of Congress Cataloging-in-Publication Data
Names: Berkner, Laurie, author. | Clanton, Ben, 1988– illustrator.
Title: Monster boogie / Laurie Berkner ; illustrated by Ben Clanton.
Description: First edition. | New York : Simon & Schuster Books for Young Readers, [2018] |
Summary: Presents a simple song about monsters and how they like to dance.
Identifiers: LCCN 2016057981| ISBN 9781481464659 (hardcover) | ISBN 9781481464666 (eBook)
Subjects: LCSH: Children's songs, English—United States—Texts. | CYAC: Monsters—Songs and
music. | Dance—Songs and music. | Songs.
Classification: LCC PZ8.3.B4558 Mon 2018 | DDC 782.42 [E]—dc23
LC record available at https://lccn.loc.gov/2016057981

LAURIE BERKNER

MONSTER BOOGIE

Illustrated by Ben Clanton

SIMON & SCHUSTER BOOKS FOR YOUNG READERS

New York   London   Toronto   Sydney   New Delhi

creak

I'm the biggest monster
that you've ever seen!

My eyes are purple

and my teeth
are green.

I'm **big** and I'm scary, you know what I mean?

And this is what I like to do. . . .

the
**monster
boogie**
round the room!

Everybody does the

monster boogie,

the
monster
boogie,

the
monster
boogie.

So can you!

'Cause I'm the biggest monster that you've ever seen!

My eyes are yellow

and my teeth are green.

I'm big and I'm hairy, you know what I mean? you know what I mean?

And this is what I like to do. . . .

the monster wiggle,

the monster wiggle

round the room!

Everybody does the monster wiggle,

the monster wiggle,

the . . .

So can you!

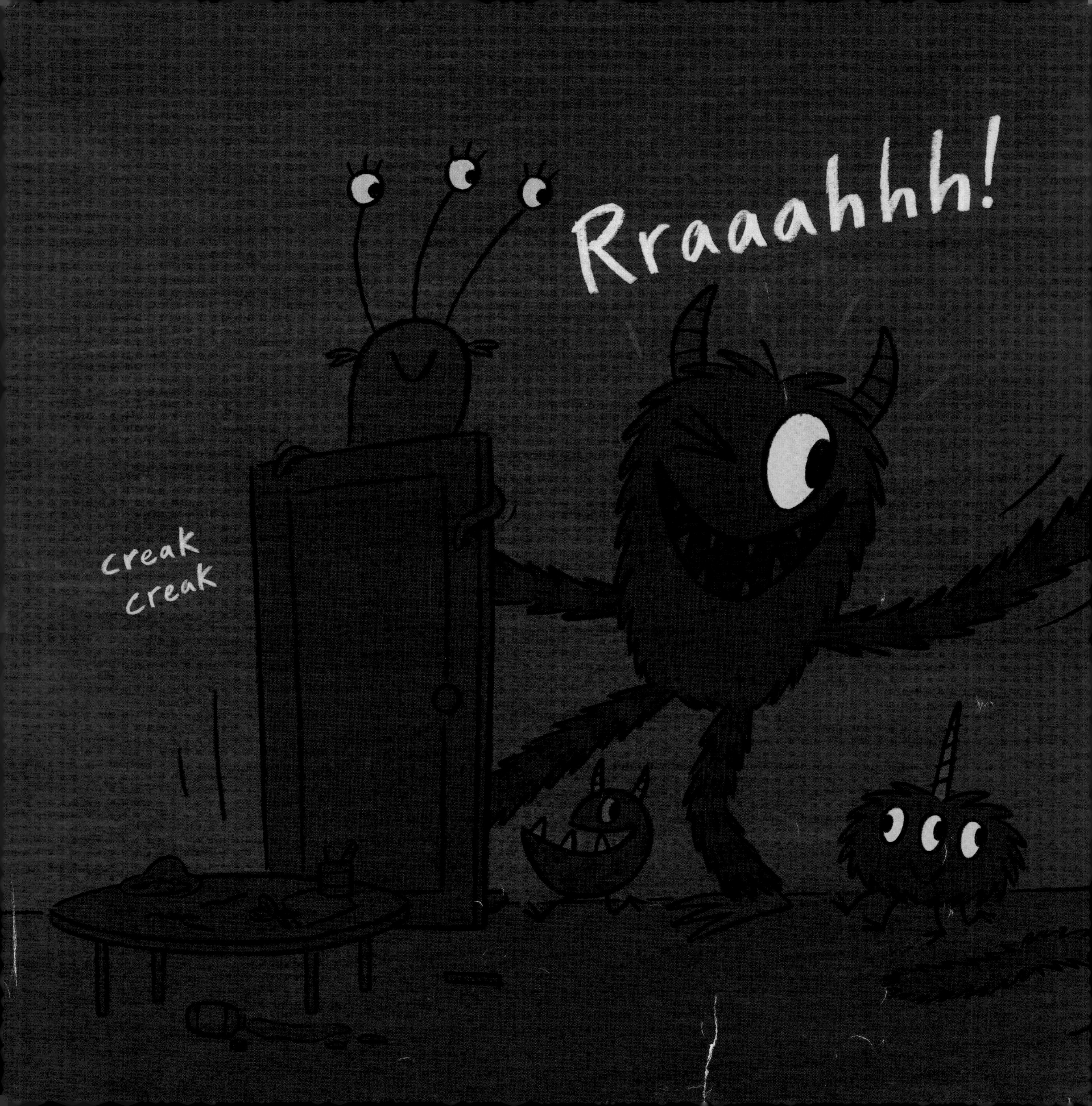
Rraaahhh!
creak
creak